ONCE-UPON-A-TIME
Story Book

By ROSE DOBBS

Illustrated by C. Walter Hodges

RANDOM HOUSE
NEW YORK

For

DEBRA,

CHARLIE,

NANCY,

MICHAEL,

LAURA,

JACQUELINE,

LISA,

ELLEN,

MARSHA,

NEIL,

and—on the other side of the Atlantic—

CRISPIN.

©Copyright, 1958, by Random House, Inc.

All rights reserved under International and Pan-American Copyright Conventions.

Published in New York by Random House, Inc.,

and simultaneously in Toronto, Canada, by Random House of Canada, Limited.

Library of Congress Catalog Card Number: 57-7523

Manufactured in the United States of America

Why Cats Always Wash Themselves
After Eating

Once upon a time a hungry cat went out to look for something special to eat. She did not want a little mouse and she did not want a saucer of milk and she did not want a juicy fishhead. She wanted something special, something different. All of a sudden she saw in front of her a little bird.

"Aha!" thought the cat. "That's exactly what I want. What a delicious meal that bird will make!"

3

So she approached softly, crouched very low, and slunk along the ground until she came close to the bird. The bird, too, was looking for something to eat, and it was so busy digging for worms that it didn't hear the cat. (Alas, that's the way things go in this world! Cats eat birds and birds eat worms and worms—but let us get on with the story.)

Suddenly the cat leaped forward and in the twinkling of an eye the bird was held fast between her paws. The poor little bird was so frightened that it was scarcely able to breathe. The cat's whiskers twitched happily as she thought of the fine meal she would soon have. But first she wanted a little fun. So she teased the bird, pushing it this way and that, pretending to let it go and snatching it back again. In the meantime, the little bird began to recover its breath and its wits.

Just as the cat opened her mouth to eat it, the bird spoke up:

"Are you going to eat me now?" it asked politely.

"Certainly," said the cat, "and it won't do you any good to object."

"Oh, I'm not objecting," said the bird. "I'm merely disappointed. It's bad enough to be eaten by a cat but it's positively humiliating to be eaten by a cat of no manners."

"No manners," cried the cat in a huff. "Who says I have no manners?"

"I have spent much time flying about," said the bird, "and I've been everywhere from the humblest cottage to the king's palace itself. Nowhere have I ever seen a cat—not even a brand-new kitten—begin a meal without washing first. It's simply out of the question in polite society."

The cat sat up proudly. "I know as well as any cat in the land," she said haughtily, "that one must wash before one eats. Now you just wait a moment." She let go of the bird and began to wash herself. Of course the bird, the moment it felt itself free, flew to safety in a nearby tree. The cat looked after it hungrily. "I deserve no better," she said to herself, "for believing so easily everything I hear."

And since that time, cats always eat first and wash afterwards.

Please All—Please None

It happened once upon a time that a man and his young son were on their way to market. With them was their donkey. And so they walked along—the donkey in the middle, the man on one side, the boy on the other.

The way was long, the sun was hot. As the three ambled on, the man and boy stopped often to wipe the sweat from their brows.

"Now aren't you two the silly ones!" exclaimed a farmer who saw them. "What is a donkey for if not to ride upon?"

So the man put his son on the donkey, and they went on.

They had not gone very far when they met several country people.

"What is the world coming to?" cried out one of them. "Have children no pity at all for their parents? Just see this great big lazy boy. He rides in comfort while his poor old father must toil in the dust and heat."

7

The man told the boy to get off and he himself got on the donkey. But they hadn't gone very far when they met a husband and wife.

"For shame," cried they. "Only a selfish father would ride on a hot day like this while his poor little son needs must trudge after."

The man stopped and scratched his head. What was he to do? Finally he took the boy up in front of him on the donkey. And they continued on their way. Soon they reached

the outskirts of the town. Everyone they met pointed fingers at them and cried, "Shame! Shame!"

"Now what is wrong?" asked the man.

"What indeed?" said the townspeople. "Anyone can see you give never a thought to the donkey. Because the poor animal cannot speak for himself, is that any reason why you and your hulking son must abuse him? How do you suppose he likes the burden of both of you on so hot a day?"

The man and the boy both jumped off the donkey. What should they do now? They thought for a long, long time, and at last an idea came to them. They cut down a pole, tied the donkey's feet to it, raised pole and donkey to their shoulders, and once more went on their way.

But at every turn they were greeted by shouts and laughter.

"See the old fool, and the young one too," cried everyone. "It's easy to tell which is the donkey in this group."

Accompanied by such remarks, the three went along until they reached a little bridge which spanned the market stream. Here the donkey, frightened by all the shouts and laughter, pulled hard at his bonds, got one of his feet loose, and kicked out. This made the boy drop his end of the pole. In the struggle that followed, the donkey fell over the bridge, into the water. As his forefeet were still tied together, he could not swim to the shore, and so he was drowned.

The man sighed sadly. "That will teach me a lesson," he said. "If you try to please everybody, you please nobody, and you lose what you have into the bargain."

The Foolish Dragon

Long, long ago, there lived a dragon in the great China sea. More than anything else in the world this dragon loved his wife. And he spent all his time granting her every wish.

One day he noticed that his wife was not looking well.

"What is it, my dear?" he asked. "What is troubling you?"

"I want something," answered she. "But I won't tell you what it is because I know you won't get it for me."

The dragon was hurt.

"Have I ever refused to get you what you want?" he asked. "Please tell me."

And he coaxed and begged so hard that at last his wife said, "I have heard that monkeys' hearts are delicious. I long to eat a monkey's heart. If I don't I know I shall die."

The poor dragon was terrified at the thought of losing his wife. But a monkey's heart! How could he ever get that?

"You know the monkeys live high in the trees, deep in the forests. How could I ever reach them?" he said.

"There," said the wife, beginning to cry. "I knew you didn't mean it when you said you'd do anything for me. You don't really care for me at all. And now I shall surely die."

The dragon didn't know what to do. Finally he said to himself, "One can only try." So he left the great China sea, went ashore, and journeyed until he came to a forest. There, 'way up in a tree, he spied a frisky monkey.

"Good afternoon, pretty one," he said, sweetly. "That is a very tall tree you're in. Aren't you afraid you'll fall out?"

"Me—fall out of a tree!" The monkey burst out laughing. "Ha, ha, ha!" he laughed. "Who ever heard of such a thing?"

The dragon saw he had made a mistake and tried again. "That isn't a very juicy-looking tree," he said, more sweetly than before. "I know a forest full of trees laden with ripe, juicy fruit. It's only across the sea."

"You are indeed a foolish dragon," said the monkey. "What you say is all very well, but how would I cross the sea?"

"Why," said the dragon innocently, "all you have to do is

get on my back, hold on tight, and I'll swim across with you."

So the little monkey came down and climbed up on the dragon's back. The dragon, of course, lost no time in striking out for the China sea. When they were halfway across, the dragon suddenly dived down beneath the water.

"Where are you going? What are you doing?" cried the monkey in alarm.

"I might as well tell you now," said the dragon. "There is no forest, there are no trees, and there is no juicy fruit. There is only my wife who is ill and who says nothing but a monkey's heart will cure her. So I am trying to drown you to get your heart for my wife."

The monkey thought fast and quick. "My dear friend," he said, "why didn't you tell me before we started out? Gladly would I give up my heart to help your wife. But don't you know that monkeys never carry their hearts around with them? I left mine in the tree where you found me. However, if you don't mind going back, I'll be happy to fetch it for you at once."

The dragon turned around and went back to the forest and the very tree where he first saw the monkey. The little monkey, with a leap and a bound, was soon safe in the topmost branch. The dragon waited and waited, and begged and begged the monkey to come down with his heart. But the monkey didn't even bother to answer him.

And for all I know that foolish dragon is still waiting there. Perhaps in time he will learn that monkeys carry with them not only their hearts but their clever thinking caps too.

The Happy Cure

A foolish king lay dying. At least, that's what he said. Yes, he said he was at death's door. But the truth of the matter was this: the king was suffering from having nothing to do. He was being bored to death.

Of course the king would not admit this. He groaned and moaned and complained of sharp stabs in every muscle and sticking pains in every bone in his body. Physicians and surgeons came from far and wide. They looked down the king's throat, they tapped his chest, and they felt his pulse. They hemmed and hawed and stroked their beards. But they could find nothing wrong.

"Physicians and surgeons are dolts!" cried the king. "Aren't there any plain ordinary doctors in the kingdom?"

The plain ordinary doctors came from hither and yon. They felt the king's pulse, tapped his chest, and looked down his throat. They hawed and hemmed, took off their spectacles, put them on again. But they could find nothing wrong.

"Plain ordinary doctors are idiots!" cried the king in a rage. "The next one who examines me and finds nothing wrong will have his ears cut off and his nose shortened."

Well, you would think that would have put a stop to the coming of the doctors and the surgeons and physicians. But no. The king kept sending messengers and couriers to bring them in. The people were in despair. Such an epidemic of heads without ears and faces with shortened noses had never been seen!

Finally a simple old woman came to see the king. The exhausted prime minister brought her into the royal bed-chamber.

The simple old woman peered into the king's face for a long time. Then she said, "Your Majesty, you are suffering from a strange and rare disease. So rare and strange, that no name exists for it."

"There, I knew it!" cried the king in glee. "I kept telling all of them, the fools, that I'm a sick man."

"A very sick man," said the simple old woman.

The king leaned back among his silken pillows and closed his eyes and wrinkled his brow as if he were in pain.

"And is there no cure for me?" he asked.

"Oh, yes, your Majesty. You need sleep but one night in the shirt of a happy man and you will be cured instantly," said the simple old woman.

The king summoned the captain of his guard and his bravest soldiers, the best couriers in the land, and the swiftest messengers and heralds.

"Start off at once," he commanded them, "and bring me back the shirt of a happy man. And mind you don't return without it," he added darkly.

The soldiers and couriers, messengers and heralds traveled far and wide from east to west, from north to south, across seas and deserts; through cities and over mountains, from one end of the kingdom to the other. But nowhere could they find a happy man. They sent long reports to the king. And this is what the reports said:

The people in the East might be happy if your Majesty didn't tax them so heavily.

And the people in the West might be happy if they didn't have to work so long and so hard, so they might have a little time to enjoy music and singing and dancing.

And the people in the North might be happy if sometimes they could see your Majesty and felt you were interested in them.

24

And the people in the South might be happy if your Majesty would notice their industry and faithfulness and would reward them.

The king read the reports hastily and flung them away. But as time went by and none of the messengers returned, and more and more reports came to him of a people that might be happy if their king so chose, he began to read more carefully.

One day a little stableboy, wandering about the palace grounds, came upon a man sitting under a tree in the royal garden. He was singing lustily.

The little stableboy approached him.

"Good afternoon," he said politely. "What makes you sing so merrily?"

"I sing from joy," said the stranger. "I love my fellow man, I own but little and want less. I am a happy man and therefore I sing."

"A happy man!" cried the little stableboy. "Oh, do you not know then that the whole kingdom is looking for you? Do you not know that the king is very ill and that only if he can sleep one night in the shirt of a happy man can he be cured? Quick, quick, take off your shirt! Quick, quick, give it to me."

26

The man burst into laughter. "My shirt," he gasped. "Why, you little ragamuffin, I don't possess a shirt." And jumping to his feet, he gathered his tattered coat about him and walked off.

The little stableboy flew to the palace. Past the guards and the prime minister he sped, right into the royal bed-chamber.

"Well, what have we here?" cried the king.

The little stableboy had to wait until he recovered his breath before he could talk.

"Oh, your Majesty," he cried. "The cure was right here all the time—right at hand—right on the palace grounds. I found him—he said he loved his fellow man, owned but little and wanted less. But," and the little boy's lips trembled, "he didn't possess a shirt."

Then the king hung his head, ashamed to meet the clear eyes of the little stableboy.

"Yes, the cure has been here all the time," he murmured. "Only I can cure my own folly."

And he resolved then and there to be a good king. He never again fancied himself ill, for he became too busy for such foolishness, and so he lived to a ripe old age.

Why The Mouse Has A Seam
In Its Face

This story happened once upon a time in the days of Noah and the Ark.

Noah, as everybody knows, had taken into his Ark two of every kind of creature, great and small. Now, one day the two little mice on board happened to sit down right next to the cat. The cat, who had been asleep, lazily opened one eye. When she saw who was sitting beside her, she opened both eyes and began to remember. She remembered that her father had always chased mice, caught them, and eaten them. And very good they were, too.

"What was good enough for my father," thought the cat, "is good enough for me." And with a leap and a bound she pounced upon one of the little mice.

The mouse ran here and there wildly, looking for a hole to hide in. But how could anyone expect to find a hole on the *Ark!* The mouse began to think she was a goner when—miracle of miracles—where not a sign of a hole had been before, a hole suddenly appeared. The mouse darted into it and quick as a flash the cat went after her. The cat was too big, of course, to get into the hole, but she put her paw in and tried to pull the mouse out.

The mouse opened her mouth very wide and the cat put her paw into the mouse's mouth. Down on the paw came the mouse's sharp teeth. The cat let out a howl of rage and clawed frantically. The little mouse opened her mouth and the cat was only too glad to escape—but not before she had clawed the mouse's cheek.

When the coast was clear, the mouse came out from the hole and went to old Noah.

"Please, kind sir," she said, "will you mend the tear in my cheek which the cat made?"

Kind old Noah took a hair from the tail of the swine and with it he carefully sewed up the tear in the mouse's cheek.

And to this very day, if you look closely you will see, right next to the mouse's mouth, a thin line in its cheek. Could this be the seam Noah made?

The Pine Tree

In a forest grew a little pine tree. Like all other pine trees his branches were covered with needles instead of with leaves. So he thought:

"These needles of mine do not please me. All the trees in the forest have pretty leaves. I, too, should like to have pretty leaves. But as it costs nothing to wish, and as long as I am wishing for leaves, I might as well wish for prettier leaves than the other trees have. Gold leaves! Ah, yes, how I should like to have leaves of gold!"

At night the little tree fell asleep and when he awoke in the morning, lo and behold! instead of slender green needles he found every single one of his branches covered with leaves of pure gold.

He was very happy.

"Now," he said proudly to himself, "I am more beautiful than any other tree in the whole forest. None of them, poor things, has such beautiful leaves as mine."

But along about noontime, a peddler with a huge sack over his shoulder wandered into the forest. The shimmering, glistening, shining golden leaves stood out from all the rest. The peddler came up to the pine tree, and when he examined the leaves and saw that they were of pure gold his joy knew no bounds. Quicker than it can be told, the peddler took his sack off his shoulder, put it on the ground, and went to work, stripping the pine tree of its golden leaves. Every one of them was stuffed into the huge sack, and when he had made sure that the tree was entirely bare, the peddler once more hoisted the sack and left the forest.

The pine tree shook and trembled while the golden leaves were being stripped. And now, as he shivered in the chill air, he cried:

"I shall never again ask for leaves of gold. Men will always rob me of them. Oh, how I should like to have leaves of glass! They could not be carried away."

At night the tree fell asleep and when he awoke in the morning, lo and behold! every one of his branches was covered with leaves of glass. They sparkled and shone in the sunlight. How beautiful they were! No other leaves in the forest were so beautiful. And our little pine tree was happy —and proud.

But along about noontime a sharp wind arose. It was a howling, growling storm wind. It whirled and swirled around the pine tree, blowing fiercely through his branches and shaking him without mercy. Every one of the glass leaves fell to the ground and broke into a thousand pieces.

Once more the pine tree was left bare, shivering in the chill air. He thought:

"Perhaps if I had ordinary green leaves, just like all the other trees in the forest, perhaps then I would be content."

At night the tree fell asleep and when he awoke in the morning, lo and behold! he was decked out in real green leaves.

But along about noontime, a frisky little goat ran into the forest and passed along by the pine tree. The goat was hungry and the juicy leaves of the pine tree were just within her reach. So she ate every single one of them. And once again the pine tree found himself bare and shivering in the chill air. And now he said to himself:

"Why did I ever wish for leaves at all? What need has a pine tree for leaves? Leaves of gold, or leaves of glass, or real leaves? Someone will always steal the golden ones; the wind will throw down and shatter the glass ones; and some animal or other will be sure to eat up real leaves. Now I see that my own needles suited me best. Oh, how I wish I had them back again!"

At night the tree fell asleep and when he awoke in the morning, lo and behold! he was dressed once more in his own slender fragrant green needles.

And now at last he was really happy. And, if the truth must be told, he was lucky, too—for suppose, just suppose that his last wish had not been granted!

The Stubborn Sillies

Now you shall hear what happened to a couple who were not only stubborn, but silly as well.

A man and wife they were, and they lived a long time ago in a cottage high on a windy hill. One evening the man had just settled himself in his rocking chair with his pipe in his mouth, and the wife had just begun to prepare supper, when a gust of wind pushed open the cottage door. It set the windows to rattling and the dishes on the cupboard shelves to dancing.

"Husband," said the woman, "get up and close the door."

"I'll do no such thing," answered he. "I didn't open it. And I'll not close it. You close it yourself."

"I didn't open it either," said the wife. "And I'll certainly not close it."

"Very well," said the husband. "You didn't open it, and I didn't open it. But whichever of us speaks first from now on shall be the one to close the door."

36

To this silly remark the wife agreed. The wind whistled in and out of the cottage. The man sat stubbornly in his chair and shivered. And the wife had all she could do to keep her teeth from chattering as she went about making supper. But neither of these silly people would close the door.

Presently the woman placed on the table a large pat of yellow butter. She poured good rich cream into a low bowl. But she did not ask her husband to come to the table. So he just sat there.

A hungry pussycat wandered by. She looked in at the open door. The man did not throw his slippers at her and the woman did not seize the broom. So the cat came in. Neither the man nor the woman cried "Scat! Scat!"—so the cat jumped up on the table and soon her little pink tongue made short work of the butter and the cream. When she had finished, the cat jumped down to the floor and began to wash herself from tail-tip to ear-tips. And still neither the man nor the woman said one word.

The woman then put on the table a platter of sizzling meat patties. And again she did not ask her husband to come and eat.

A large hungry dog came sniffing along. How good the patties smelled! With one leap the dog was in the cottage. Neither the man nor the woman said a single word, so the dog jumped up on the table and *gulp! gulp!*—there was an end to all the meat. Feeling very good, the dog licked his chops, jumped down to the floor, turned around and around and around and soon was fast asleep in a big furry ball. And still neither the man nor the woman said one word.

Then the woman put on the table a fresh cherry pie and a big pitcher of warm milk. And still she didn't ask her husband to come and eat.

A thief came along. He poked his head in at the open door. The man and the woman made no move. The thief stepped cautiously into the cottage. All remained quiet. The thief then sat down at the table and quicker than it takes to tell, he ate up the whole pie and drank all the milk. Then he gathered all the spoons and knives and forks together and put them into his pouch.

"These two must be deaf and dumb and blind," he said to himself. "Now, let's see. What else can I take?"

His eyes went around the room and soon spotted the woman's best china teapot.

"Now, there's something," he said aloud. "That should fetch me a pretty penny."

He went over to the cupboard and reached for the teapot. But at this the woman burst out at the top of her lungs:

"Vagabond! Rogue! Thief! Isn't it enough that you have eaten the whole pie and drunk all the milk and stolen all our silver? Must you have my best teapot too?"

Her cries so startled the cat and dog that both jumped to their feet, the cat hissing and spitting and the dog growling and barking. As for the thief, he was so astonished at all the sudden noise that he was frightened out of his wits. He dropped the teapot, clutched the silver tightly to him, and took to his heels. Out the open door he sped, with the cat and the dog in pursuit.

"After them, man!" cried the woman. "Will you sit there and do nothing while we lose everything?"

But the stubborn silly man, with all the food gone, the silver stolen, and the best teapot in a thousand pieces on the floor, only shrugged his shoulders and said:

"Wife, you spoke first. Now go and close the door."

The Bird And The Hunter

A hunter once upon a time spent a whole day in the forest but luck was not with him. He caught nothing until, late in the day, just as he was about to leave, he came upon a bird sleeping in its nest. The hunter seized the bird who woke up and, to the man's surprise, began to talk.

"Let me go, Hunter," it said. "As you can see, I'm nearly all feathers. I'll hardly make you a decent meal. But if you do let me go, I will give you three pieces of wisdom. If you guard them carefully and live by them, you will be hand-somely rewarded."

The hunter was curious to know what the pieces of wisdom might be, so he promised to let the bird go; but first, he said, he was to be given the three pieces of wisdom.

"Very well," said the bird. "Here is the first: Never believe any story that your common sense tells you cannot be true. And here is the second: When you have made a decision, abide by it and do not at once regret having made it. And the third is: Never try to do the impossible."

The hunter was a little disappointed. "This wisdom of yours," he said, "is only ordinary advice, the kind I've known all my life. It hasn't ever brought me any reward, though."

"Knowing good advice and abiding by it are two different things," replied the bird. "And now, keep your promise and let me go."

So the hunter let the bird go and off it flew and perched on a low branch of a nearby tree. From there it looked down at the hunter mockingly.

"Oh, what a fool you are," it said. "Do you suppose I am a common bird? Oh no, I'm special. And do you know why? Not, as you may think, because I can talk—many birds can do that—but because of the claws on my right leg. Didn't you notice them? How they glitter and shine? They aren't claws at all but jewels so rare there are none like them in all the world. Had you killed me and taken these jewels, they would have made you rich beyond your wildest dreams."

Not for a moment did the hunter doubt this fantastic story. At once he regretted letting the bird go and immedi-

ately went after it. The bird flew to a higher branch. The hunter leaped up, grasped the branch, and tried to hoist himself up. But the branch cracked under his weight and before he knew it he crashed to the ground, and lay there badly shaken. The little bird mocked him again.

"You see, there is a difference between knowing good advice and following it," it said. "In these few minutes you have completely forgotten all three pieces of wisdom.

"First, you believed my silly story. Doesn't your common sense tell you no living bird could have jewels for claws? Second, you no sooner let me go than you regretted it. And third, what made you, clumsy man, think you could do the impossible? Did you hope to catch with your bare hands a bird in flight? Ponder well these pieces of wisdom, foolish one, and try to live by them in the future."

And the bird flew away.

Rising painfully to his feet, the hunter limped out of the forest, a sad but wiser man.

The Wise King And The Little Bee

Many, many years ago there lived in the holy city of Jerusalem a mighty king whose name was Solomon. And his fame was in all the nations round about. For God had given Solomon a wise and understanding heart. He was wiser than any man who lived before him and any man who came after. And all the earth sought the presence of Solomon to hear his wisdom, and he always judged wisely and well.

Now, suppose I were to tell you that a little bee—a little, tiny, insignificant bee—once proved itself to be wiser than this wisest of men? You would probably not believe it. Yet it is true. There is an old, old story to prove it, and because Solomon was as humble as he was wise, the story has a happy ending. And here it is:

It happened that among the countries which rang with the fame of Solomon's wisdom and riches was the country over which ruled the proud and beautiful Queen of Sheba. She longed to prove to everyone that Solomon was not the wisest man in the world.

"If only," she said to herself, "I could set him some difficult task which he could not perform—or, better still, ask him a simple question which he would not be able to answer!" She thought and she thought and at last an idea came to her.

She called together all the most skilled craftsmen in the land, and she commanded them to fashion for her a bouquet of flowers. It was to be of roses of Sharon and lilies of the valley. And the flowers were to be made so beautifully, so perfectly, that no one standing within a few inches of them would be able to tell that they were not real. The craftsmen went to work and shortly afterwards brought the bouquet to the Queen. The little bells of the lilies of the valley and the purple blossoms of the roses of Sharon were so perfect that the Queen could not believe they were not real. And her skilled workmen had labored long and hard to distill a perfume that matched perfectly the fragrance of the real flowers.

The Queen was more than pleased. "Now we shall see," said she, "how wise Solomon truly is."

So she announced that she would pay him a visit; to do him honor, she said. And she came to Jerusalem with a very great train, with camels that bore spices and much gold, and with boxes full of precious stones.

Solomon received her graciously. The best rooms in the palace were offered to her and her companions. The finest musicians and dancers entertained her. And a lavish banquet was planned for her.

On the evening of the banquet, the Queen sent her most
trusted servant to procure a bouquet of real roses of Sharon
and lilies of the valley. When the merry-making and feasting
were in full swing, the Queen left the gay company and soon
returned with the two bouquets. Everyone gasped. Never had
there been seen such beautiful bouquets, such perfect flowers,
and one the exact copy of the other.

"O, great and mighty King," said the Queen of Sheba,
standing at a little distance from Solomon and holding out
the two bouquets, "the whole world rings with stories of your
wisdom. Tell me, you who can always see the truth, which of
these bouquets is made up of real flowers and which of false?"

There was a deep silence in the vast hall. Not one person
there could see any difference between the two bouquets. The

55

little white bells of the lilies of the valley swayed gently in each and the lovely purple blossoms of the roses of Sharon sent out a faint perfume from each.

The deep silence was broken by a whispering and murmuring which started in one corner, traveled to another and soon filled the vast hall. Solomon leaned forward and wrinkled his brow. He heard the excited and anxious mutterings of his people, but both bouquets looked exactly alike. Perhaps they were both real? Or, perhaps they were both false? Suddenly, above the hum in the hall, Solomon's sharp ear caught another sound. It was made by a little bee buzzing against a window. Solomon smiled. He was wise enough to know that all wisdom comes from God and that God has given to each of His creatures a special wisdom of its own. So he motioned to one of his servants to open the window. No sooner was this done than the bee flew into the room. The King's eyes followed it. Straight and sure it flew to one of the bouquets and was soon lost to sight deep within the blossoms. So engrossed in watching the Queen or in whispering to one another were the people that no one noticed what had happened.

The King sat up very straight and met the Queen's mocking eyes.

"My gracious and honored guest," he said, "the true flowers are those," and he pointed to the bouquet chosen by the little bee.

The Queen was astonished. Then she smiled and bowed.

"It was a true report that I heard in my own land of your acts and of your wisdom," she said. "But I did not believe the words until I came and saw for myself. You have wisdom beyond the fame of which I have heard. Happy are your men, happy are your servants, happy are all those who stand before you always and hear your wisdom."

Then a great shout and roar of praise rang out from all the people. But the King himself was silent. In his heart he was giving thanks for the little bee that had come to help him.

The Teeny Tiny Omelet

Once upon a time there was a teeny tiny old woman who lived in a teeny tiny old house. She had a teeny tiny hen and one day the hen laid a teeny tiny egg.

"Oh, thank you very much," said the teeny tiny old woman. "I shall have a fine breakfast today."

With a bit of butter and a few drops of milk and the egg she made herself an omelet. But when she went to eat it, she found that it was too hot, so she put it on the window sill to cool.

"Buzzzz . . . Buzzzz . . . Buzzzz!" Along came a fly and *snap!* he ate up the omelet. Just like that. Can you *imagine* what a teeny tiny omelet it was?

Furious at the fly, the little old woman put on her bonnet and went off to the police station.

"Good morning, granny," said the policeman at the door. "What can I do for you?"

The little old woman told him about her omelet and the fly who ate it up and she demanded that the fly be arrested.

The policeman laughed and laughed. "No omelet can be that tiny," he said, "and who ever heard of arresting a fly? I have no time for such nonsense. Please go away."

But the little old woman would not go away, so the policeman sent her to the sergeant.

"Good morning, granny," said the sergeant. "Can I do anything for you?"

The little old woman told the sergeant about her omelet and the fly that ate it up. "I want that fly arrested at once," she said.

The sergeant laughed and laughed. "No omelet can be that tiny," he said, "and who ever heard of arresting a fly? I'm much too busy for such nonsense. Go away, please."

But the little old woman would not go away, so the sergeant telephoned the captain.

"Sir," he said, "I have here a citizen who reports a robbery and demands that an immediate arrest be made."

"Then make it," snapped the captain.

"Oh, but the thief is something out of the ordinary and will take some catching," said the sergeant. "I'm afraid the case is too hard for me to handle."

"I'm not surprised!" The captain, a proud and vain man, spoke sarcastically. "Any real work around here always has to be done by me. Send the citizen in."

Although he was somewhat startled to find that the citizen was a teeny tiny old woman, he listened to her story. When she had finished, he said to himself, "What nonsense! But I'll get rid of her."

Then he told the little old woman that she was quite right. "The thief should be punished," he said, "but arresting him isn't enough. He must be taught a lesson. So here is a stout club. When next you see the fly, give him a good hard whack."

The captain leaned over to hand her the club, and just then a fly alighted on his nose. The little old woman thought it was the same fly that had eaten up her omelet. So—*whack!* she brought the club down on the fly!

"Owww! Ouch!" yelled the captain, dancing up and down and holding his aching nose.

"Serves you right," said the teeny tiny old woman, thinking it was the fly yelling. Then she straightened her bonnet and went home, quite satisfied that she had properly punished the fly who ate up her teeny tiny omelet.

Other titles in this series

Published by

RANDOM HOUSE, 457 MADISON AVENUE, NEW YORK 22, N.Y.

ONCE-
UPON-A-TIME
Story Book

The Bird and the

Hunter

The
Wise
King
and the
Little
Be

The

Jeen